Dennis is a very poor student at the Dragon School until he has an exciting dream. Then he becomes a true, flame-throwing dragon. When Dennis leaves school and looks for work, his fire and flames make him a very popular and useful young dragon throughout the town. These two stories about Dennis the Dragon are told in rhyme and are boldly and amusingly illustrated in full colour to delight all young children.

Dennis
the
Dragon

by VERA HOPEWELL

illustrated by MARTIN AITCHISON

Ladybird Books Loughborough

Dennis was the dearest dragon,
Mrs Dragon's youngest son.
All the other boys were naughty.
Dennis was the dreamy one.

When at school, the dragon teacher
Showed them how to breathe out flame,
All the boys did well but Dennis.
How he hung his head in shame.

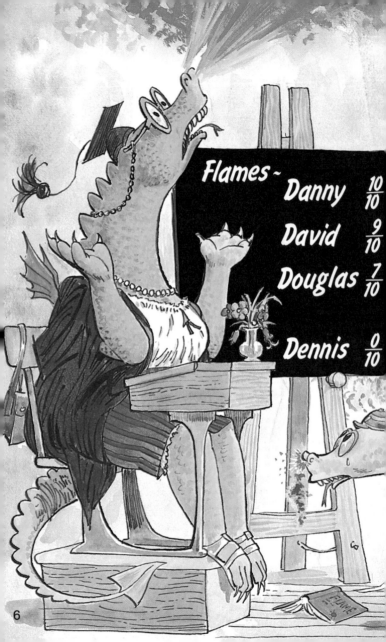

Flames ~
Danny $\frac{10}{10}$
David $\frac{9}{10}$
Douglas $\frac{7}{10}$

Dennis $\frac{0}{10}$

6

All he managed was a little,
Tiny, feeble, smoky puff.
Teacher Dragon was quite cross and
Said that this was not enough.

Dennis tried so very hard but
Flames just simply wouldn't come.
All the boys just laughed at Dennis,
Called him names like "soft" and "dumb".

Dennis crept away so sadly.

All he needed was to weep.

So he cried, and then he curled up,

Drifted slowly off to sleep.

Fast asleep he saw a vision.

First there was a lot of steam.

Dennis couldn't understand it;

Didn't know it was a dream!

Then out from the steam there came
A lovely little dragon girl.
Oh! She was so very pretty,
Eyes like diamonds, teeth like pearl.

Oh! How Dennis wished he knew her!

Talk to her he didn't dare.

Then he heard a noise like thunder,

Awful roarings filled the air!

From the steam there came a frightful,
Huge and ugly, dragon boy.
All that steam was smoke he'd puffed out,
Simply seeking to annoy.

When he saw the pretty girl there,
He came rushing to the spot.
She was frightened; who could blame her?
Strangely, Dennis just was not!

Well before the baddy reached her
He rushed forward; stood in front.
If the baddy tried to touch her,
He'd stay there and bear the brunt.

As the baddy bounded forward,
Dennis shouted, "I am game.
I will fight you if I have to."
Then he saw some puffs of flame.

Suddenly he knew, that he had
Puffed them as he'd mounted guard.
All at once it was so easy.
Had he ever thought it hard?

Now he knew that he could do it
Just like grown-up dragon men,
And he knew that he would never
Find it hard to do again.

Then he saw that baddy Dragon,

Turning on his tail to flee.

"Goodness!" thought our Dennis, staggered.

"Can it be he's scared of me?"

And he *was*! Away he hurried,
Fading through the thinning smoke.
Then at that exciting moment,
Dennis from his sleep awoke!

Where, oh where, the pretty maiden?
Had the baddy gone at last?
Dennis was confused, bewildered,
But his dream was fading fast.

Suddenly, one thing he thought of.
In his dream he'd puffed a flame.
So he had another try and
The result was just the same!

"I can do it! I can do it!"
Dennis shouted, in his joy.
"I am just the same as others.
I'm a proper dragon boy!"

Then along came all the others
On their way to dragon school.
"I'll just show them," Dennis murmured.
"Mustn't rush it — play it cool."

So as they all wandered past him,
He just stood there, head in air.
Gave a little puff and snort and
Smoke and flames were everywhere!

How the others stood and wondered!
Dennis simply wouldn't tell!
The Teacher Dragon was so pleased,
She gave a star for doing well.

Dennis
Goes to Work

Dennis was a few years older.
Had to leave the dragon school.
Time for him to earn a living.
No more time to dream or fool.

Mrs Dragon hid her tears
As Dennis set off down the lane.
Would he find a job to suit him?
Would she see her son again?

His head was filled with fancy dreams
As Dennis walked throughout the day.
But then the sun began to fade and
Dennis knew he'd lost his way.

Dennis didn't like the night-time,
Didn't want to be alone.
Then he saw some distant town lights,
Rushed towards this place unknown.

He knocked politely on the first door
Hoping he might find a place.
The door was opened by a big man,
Covered in flour, grumpy face.

He was the baker for the whole town.
Things were not all going well.
When he saw that it was Dennis,
In disappointment, his face fell.

"Well, young dragon, what's the matter?
I've no time to stand and chat.
My old ovens have just gone out.
All my bread is going flat."

"I was looking for some lodgings,"
Dennis said, quite nervously.
"But I think that I can help you.
Come with me and we shall see."

They both went and found the ovens.
"Stand well back, please," Dennis said.
Then he huffed and puffed and blew a
Giant flame to bake the bread.

Soon the loaves were browning nicely.

Mr Baker danced for joy.

"You have saved my baking business.

A thousand thanks, young dragon boy."

Dennis sat there quite embarrassed.

Didn't know quite what to say.

Then he ventured, very shyly,

"If you like, sir, I could stay."

News of Dennis and the baker
Soon was spreading far and wide.
People queued for loaves of bread
And many had to wait outside.

Dennis got up every morning,
Blew his fire to bake the bread.
Worked all day to help the baker
And tired but happy, went to bed.

Now the people knew the dragon,
Liked his happy, smiling face.
So they asked if he could do some
Other jobs around the place.

One November, cold and rainy,
The town's big bonfire wouldn't catch.
"Send for Dennis," someone shouted.
"He'd be better than a match."

Dennis looked at their wet bonfire.
Then he blew his biggest flame.
Soon the fire was burning brightly.
Bonfire night seemed just the same.

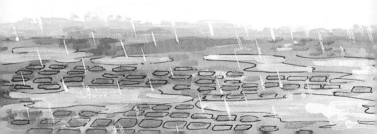

40

"Thank you, Dennis," said the children.
"Come and watch our rockets fly."
Dennis liked to watch the fireworks,
Banging, sparkling in the sky.

Dennis Dragon roasted chestnuts,
Sausages, potatoes too.
Thanks to Dennis, this became the
Best Bonfire night they all knew.

Mr Baker said to Dennis,
"Christmas will be coming next."
The dragon hadn't thought of Christmas,
Stood there looking quite perplexed!

The baker talked to him about it,
As they worked throughout the nights.
"We sing carols and give presents,
And have Christmas trees with lights."

"Jesus Christ was born at Christmas
And we celebrate each year."
That this was something very special,
To Dennis soon became quite clear.

The baker made more bread than ever.
Soon their flour was getting low.
Dennis looked out of the window,
To find it had begun to snow.

By next day the snow was deeper,
Roads were blocked and cars were stuck,
And the flour the baker needed,
Wouldn't come without some luck.

"No bread tomorrow," said the baker,
And he seemed so very sad.
Dennis thought, until he found the
Best idea he'd ever had.

Out into the snow marched Dennis.

It was cold for dragon toes.

Then he breathed and puffed quite gently,

Till a flame came from his nose.

With dragon flames, the snow was melting
And this cleared the snow-blocked road.
A truck was soon at Mr Baker's,
Delivering its flour load.

By Christmas Day, the work was over.
Time for holidays had come.
"Just a few days off," said Dennis.
"I'd like to go and visit Mum."

49

Mrs Dragon, hugging Dennis,
Was so pleased to see her son.
Proudly then he told his mother
All about the work he'd done.

51

DENNIS the DRAGON